The Adventure of the Christmas Pudding

by
Agatha Christie

The Sketch, December 12, 1923

The Adventure of the Christmas Pudding

I

"I regret exceedingly–" said M. Hercule Poirot.

He was interrupted. Not rudely interrupted. The interruption was suave, dexterous, persuasive rather than contradictory.

"Please don't refuse offhand, M. Poirot. There are grave issues of State. Your co-operation will be appreciated in the highest quarters."

"You are too kind," Hercule Poirot waved a hand, "but I really cannot undertake to do as you ask. At this season of the year –"

Again Mr Jesmond interrupted. "Christmas time," he said, persuasively. "An old-fashioned Christmas in the English countryside."

Hercule Poirot shivered. The thought of the English countryside at this season of the year did not attract him.

"A good old-fashioned Christmas!" Mr Jesmond stressed it.

"Me–I am not an Englishman," said Hercule Poirot. "In my country, Christmas, it is for the children. The New Year, that is what we celebrate."

"Ah," said Mr Jesmond, "but Christmas in England is a great institution and I assure you at Kings Lacey you would see it at its best. It's a wonderful old house, you know. Why, one wing of it dates from the fourteenth century."

Again Poirot shivered. The thought of a fourteenth-century English manor house filled him with apprehension. He had suffered too often in the historic country houses of England. He looked round appreciatively at his comfortable modern flat with its radiators and the latest patent devices for excluding any kind of draught.

"In the winter," he said firmly, "I do not leave London."

"I don't think you quite appreciate, M. Poirot, what a very serious matter this is." Mr Jesmond glanced at his companion and then back at Poirot. Poirot's second visitor had up to now said nothing but a polite and formal "How do you do." He sat now, gazing down at his well-polished shoes, with an air of the utmost dejection on his coffee-coloured face. He was a young man, not more than twenty-three, and he was clearly in a state of complete misery.

"Yes, yes," said Hercule Poirot. "Of course the matter is serious. I do appreciate that. His Highness has my heartfelt sympathy."

"The position is one of the utmost delicacy," said Mr Jesmond.

Poirot transferred his gaze from the young man to his older companion. If one wanted to sum up Mr Jesmond in a word, the word would have been discretion. Everything about Mr Jesmond was discreet. His well-cut but inconspicuous clothes, his pleasant, well-bred voice which rarely soared out of an agreeable monotone, his light-brown hair just thinning a little at the temples, his pale serious face. It seemed to Hercule Poirot that he had known not one Mr Jesmond but a dozen Mr Jesmonds in his time, all using sooner or later the same phrase–"a position of the utmost delicacy". "The police," said Hercule Poirot, "can be very discreet, you know."

Mr Jesmond shook his head firmly.

"Not the police," he said. "To recover the–er–what we want to recover will almost inevitably invoke taking proceedings in the law courts and we know so little. We suspect, but we do not know."

"You have my sympathy," said Hercule Poirot again. If he imagined that his sympathy was going to mean anything to his two visitors, he was wrong. They did not want sympathy, they wanted practical help. Mr Jesmond began once more to talk about the delights of an English Christmas.

"It's dying out, you know," he said, "the real old-fashioned type of Christmas. People spend it at hotels nowadays. But an English Christmas with all the family gathered round, the children and their stockings, the Christmas tree, the turkey and plum pudding, the crackers. The snowman outside the window–"

In the interests of exactitude, Hercule Poirot intervened.

"To make a snowman one has to have the snow," he remarked severely. "And one cannot have snow to order, even for an English Christmas."

"I was talking to a friend of mine in the meteorological office only today," said Mr Jesmond, "and he tells me that it is highly probable there will be snow this Christmas."

It was the wrong thing to have said. Hercule Poirot shuddered more forcefully than ever.

"Snow in the country!" he said. "That would be still more abominable. A large, cold, stone manor house."

"Not at all," said Mr Jesmond. "Things have changed very much in the last ten years or so. Oil-fired central heating."

"They have oil-fired central heating at Kings Lacey?" asked Poirot. For the first time he seemed to waver.

Mr Jesmond seized his opportunity. "Yes, indeed," he said, "and a splendid hot water system. Radiators in every bedroom. I assure you, my dear M. Poirot, Kings Lacey is comfort itself in the winter time. You might even find the house too warm."

"That is most unlikely," said Hercule Poirot.

With practised dexterity Mr Jesmond shifted his ground a little. "You can appreciate the terrible dilemma we are in," he said, in a confidential manner.

Hercule Poirot nodded. The problem was, indeed, not a happy one. A young potentate-to-be, the only son of the ruler of a rich and important native State, had arrived in London a few weeks ago. His country had been passing through a period of restlessness and discontent. Though loyal to the father whose way of life had remained persistently Eastern, popular opinion was somewhat dubious of the younger generation. His follies had been Western ones and as such looked upon with disapproval.

Recently, however, his betrothal had been announced. He was to marry a cousin of the same blood, a young woman who, though educated at Cambridge, was careful to display no Western influence in her own country. The wedding day was announced and the young prince had made a journey to England, bringing with him some of the famous jewels of his house to be reset in appropriate modern settings by Cartier. These had included a very famous ruby which had been removed from its cumbersome old-fashioned necklace and had been given a new look by the famous jewellers. So far so good, but after this came the snag. It was not to be supposed that a young man possessed of much wealth and convivial tastes, should not commit a few follies of the pleasanter type. As to that there would have been no censure. Young princes were supposed to amuse themselves in this fashion. For the prince to take the girl friend of the moment for a walk down Bond Street and bestow upon her an emerald bracelet or a diamond clip as a reward for the pleasure she had afforded him would have been regarded as quite natural and suitable, corresponding in fact to the Cadillac cars which his father invariably presented to his favourite dancing girl of the moment. But the prince had been far more indiscreet than that. Flattered by the lady's interest, he had displayed to her the famous ruby in its new setting, and had finally been so unwise as to accede to her request to be allowed to wear it–just for one evening!

The sequel was short and sad. The lady had retired from their supper table to powder her nose. Time passed. She did not return. She had left the establishment by another door and since then had disappeared into space.

The important and distressing thing was that the ruby in its new setting had disappeared with her.

These were the facts that could not possibly be made public without the most dire consequences. The ruby was something more than a ruby, it was a historical possession of

7

great significance, and the circumstances of its disappearance were such that any undue publicity about them might result in the most serious political consequences.

Mr Jesmond was not the man to put these facts into simple language. He wrapped them up, as it were, in a great deal of verbiage. Who exactly Mr Jesmond was, Hercule Poirot did not know. He had met other Mr Jesmonds in the course of his career. Whether he was connected with the Home Office, the Foreign Secretary or some other discreet branch of public service was not specified. He was acting in the interests of the Commonwealth. The ruby must be recovered.

M. Poirot, so Mr Jesmond delicately insisted, was the man to recover it.

"Perhaps–yes," Hercule Poirot admitted, "but you can tell me so little. Suggestion–suspicion–all that is not very much to go upon."

"Come now, Monsieur Poirot, surely it is not beyond your powers. Ah, come now."

"I do not always succeed."

But this was mock modesty. It was clear enough from Poirot's tone that for him to undertake a mission was almost synonymous with succeeding in it.

"His Highness is very young," Mr Jesmond said. "It will be sad if his whole life is to be blighted for a mere youthful indiscretion." Poirot looked kindly at the downcast young man. "It is the time for follies, when one is young," he said encouragingly, "and for the ordinary young man it does not matter so much. The good papa, he pays up; the family lawyer, he helps to disentangle the inconvenience; the young man, he learns by experience and all ends for the best. In a position such as yours, it is hard indeed. Your approaching marriage–"

"That is it. That is it exactly." For the first time words poured from the young man. "You see she is very, very serious. She takes life very seriously. She has acquired at Cambridge many very serious ideas. There is to be education in my country. There are to be schools. There are to be many things. All in the name of progress, you understand, of democracy. It will not be, she says, like it was in my father"s time. Naturally she knows that I will have diversions in London, but not the scandal. No! It is the scandal that matters. You see it is very, very famous, this ruby. There is a long trail behind it, a history. Much bloodshed–many deaths!"

"Deaths," said Hercule Poirot thoughtfully. He looked at Mr Jesmond.

"One hopes," he said, "it will not come to that?"

Mr Jesmond made a peculiar noise rather like a hen who has decided to lay an egg and then thought better of it.

"No, no indeed," he said, sounding rather prim. "There is no question, I am sure, of anything of that kind."

"You cannot be sure," said Hercule Poirot. "Whoever has the ruby now, there may be others who want to gain possession of it, and who will not stick at a trifle, my friend."

"I really don't think," said Mr Jesmond, sounding more prim than ever, "that we need enter into speculation of that kind. Quite unprofitable."

"Me," said Hercule Poirot, suddenly becoming very foreign, "me, I explore all the avenues, like the politicians."

Mr Jesmond looked at him doubtfully. Pulling himself together, he said, "Well, I can take it that is settled, M. Poirot? You will go to Kings Lacey?"

"And how do I explain myself there?" asked Hercule Poirot.

Mr Jesmond smiled with confidence.

"That, I think, can be arranged very easily," he said. "I can assure you that it will all seem quite natural. You will find the Laceys most charming. Delightful people."

"And you do not deceive me about the oil-fired central heating?"

"No, no, indeed." Mr Jesmond sounded quite pained. "I assure you you will find every comfort."

"Tout confort moderne," murmured Poirot to himself, reminiscently. "Eh bien," he said, "I accept."

II

The temperature in the long drawing-room at Kings Lacey was a comfortable sixty-eight as Hercule Poirot sat talking to Mrs Lacey by one of the big mullioned windows. Mrs Lacey was engaged in needlework. She was not doing petit point or embroidered flowers upon silk. Instead, she appeared to be engaged in the prosaic task of hemming dishcloths. As she sewed she talked in a soft reflective voice that Poirot found very charming.

"I hope you will enjoy our Christmas party here, M. Poirot. It's only the family, you know. My granddaughter and a grandson and a friend of his and Bridget who's my great niece, and Diana who's a cousin and David Welwyn who is a very old friend. Just a family party. But Edwina Morecombe said that that's what you really wanted to see. An old-fashioned Christmas. Nothing could be more old-fashioned than we are! My husband, you know, absolutely lives in the past. He likes everything to be just as it was when he was a boy of twelve years old, and used to come here for his holidays." She smiled to herself. "All the same old things, the Christmas tree and the stockings hung up and the oyster soup and the turkey—two turkeys, one boiled and one roast— and the plum pudding with the ring and the bachelor's button and all the rest of it in it. We can't have sixpences nowadays because they're not pure silver any more. But all the old desserts, the Elvas plums and Carlsbad plums and almonds and raisins, and crystallized fruit and ginger. Dear me, I sound like a catalogue from Fortnum and Mason!"

"You arouse my gastronomic juices, Madame."

"I expect we'll all have frightful indigestion by tomorrow evening," said Mrs Lacey. "One isn't used to eating so much nowadays, is one?"

She was interrupted by some loud shouts and whoops of laughter outside the window. She glanced out.

"I don't know what they're doing out there. Playing some game or other, I suppose. I've always been so afraid, you know, that these young people would be bored by our Christmas here. But not at all, it's just the opposite. Now my own son and daughter and their friends, they used to be rather sophisticated about Christmas. Say it was all nonsense and too much fuss and it would be far better to go out to a hotel somewhere and dance. But the younger generation seem to find all this terribly attractive. Besides," added Mrs Lacey practically, "schoolboys and schoolgirls are always hungry, aren't they? I think they must starve them at these schools. After all, one does know children of that age each eat about as much as three strong men."

Poirot laughed and said, "It is most kind of you and your husband, Madame, to include me in this way in your family party."

"Oh, we're both delighted, I'm sure," said Mrs Lacey. "And if you find Horace a little gruff," she continued, "pay no attention. It's just his manner, you know."

What her husband, Colonel Lacey, had actually said was: "Can't think why you want one of these damned foreigners here cluttering up Christmas? Why can't we have him some other time? Can't stick foreigners! All right, all right, so Edwina Morecombe wished him on us. What's it got to do with her, I should like to know? Why doesn't she have him for Christmas?"

"Because you know very well," Mrs Lacey had said, "that Edwina always goes to Claridge's."

Her husband had looked at her piercingly and said, "Not up to something, are you, Em?"

"Up to something?" said Em, opening very blue eyes. "Of course not. Why should I be?"

Old Colonel Lacey laughed, a deep, rumbling laugh. "I wouldn't put it past you, Em," he said. "When you look your most innocent is when you are up to something."

Revolving these things in her mind, Mrs Lacey went on: "Edwina said she thought perhaps you might help us . . . I'm sure I don't know quite how, but she said that friends of yours had once found you very helpful in–in a case something like ours. I–well, perhaps you don't know what I'm talking about?"

Poirot looked at her encouragingly. Mrs Lacey was close on seventy, as upright as a ramrod, with snow-white hair, pink cheeks, blue eyes, a ridiculous nose and a determined chin.

"If there is anything I can do I shall only be too happy to do it," said Poirot. "It is, I understand, a rather unfortunate matter of a young girl's infatuation."

Mrs Lacey nodded. "Yes. It seems extraordinary that I should–well, want to talk to you about it. After all, you are a perfect stranger . . ."

"And a foreigner," said Poirot, in an understanding manner.

"Yes," said Mrs Lacey, "but perhaps that makes it easier, in a way. Anyhow, Edwina seemed to think that you might perhaps know something–how shall I put it–something useful about this young Desmond Lee-Wortley."

Poirot paused a moment to admire the ingenuity of Mr Jesmond and the ease with which he had made use of Lady Morecombe to further his own purposes.

"He has not, I understand, a very good reputation, this young man?" he began delicately.

"No, indeed, he hasn't! A very bad reputation! But that's no help so far as Sarah is concerned. It's never any good, is it, telling young girls that men have a bad reputation? It–it just spurs them on!"

"You are so very right," said Poirot.

"In my young day," went on Mrs Lacey. ("Oh dear, that's a very long time ago!) We used to be warned, you know, against certain young men, and of course it did heighten one's interest in them, and if one could possibly manage to dance with them, or to be alone with them in a dark conservatory–" She laughed. "That's why I wouldn't let Horace do any of the things he wanted to do."

"Tell me," said Poirot, "exactly what is it that troubles you?"

"Our son was killed in the war," said Mrs Lacey. "My daughter-in-law died when Sarah was born so that she has always been with us, and we've brought her up. Perhaps we've brought her up unwisely–I don't know. But we thought we ought always to leave her as free as possible."

"That is desirable, I think," said Poirot. "One cannot go against the spirit of the times."

"No," said Mrs Lacey, "that's just what I felt about it. And, of course, girls nowadays do these sort of things."

Poirot looked at her inquiringly.

"I think the way one expresses it," said Mrs Lacey, "is that Sarah has got in with what they call the coffee-bar set. She won't go to dances or come out properly or be a deb or anything of that kind. Instead she has two rather unpleasant rooms in Chelsea down by the river and wears these funny clothes that they like to wear, and black stockings or bright green ones. Very thick stockings. (So prickly, I always think!) And she goes about without washing or combing her hair."

"Ça, c'est tout à fait naturelle," said Poirot. "It is the fashion of the moment. They grow out of it."

"Yes, I know," said Mrs Lacey. "I wouldn't worry about that sort of thing. But you see she's taken up with this Desmond Lee-Wortley and he really has a very unsavoury reputation. He lives more or less on well-to-do girls. They seem to go quite mad about him. He very nearly married the Hope girl, but her people got her made a ward in court or something. And of course that's what Horace wants to do. He says he must do it for her protection. But I don't think it"s really a good idea, M. Poirot. I mean, they'll just run away together and go to Scotland or Ireland or the Argentine or somewhere and either get married or else live together without getting married. And although it may be contempt of court and all that–well, it isn't really an answer, is it, in the end? Especially if a baby's coming. One has to give in then, and let them get married. And then, nearly always, it seems to me, after a year or two there's a divorce. And then the girl comes home and usually after a year or two she marries someone so nice he's almost dull and settles down. But it's particularly sad, it seems to me, if there is a child, because it's not the same thing, being brought up by a stepfather, however nice. No, I think it's much better if we did as we did in my young days. I mean the first young man one fell in love with was always someone undesirable. I remember I had a horrible passion for a young man called–now what was his name now?–how strange it is, I can't remember his Christian name at all! Tibbitt, that was his surname. Young Tibbitt. Of course, my father more or less forbade him the house, but he used to get asked to the same dances, and we used to dance together. And sometimes we'd escape and sit out together and occasionally friends would arrange picnics to which we both went. Of course, it was all very exciting and forbidden and one enjoyed it enormously. But one didn't go to the–well, to the lengths that girls go nowadays. And so, after a while, the Mr Tibbitts faded out. And do you know, when I saw him four years later I was surprised what I could ever have seen in him! He seemed to be such a dull young man. Flashy, you know. No interesting conversation."

"One always thinks the days of one's own youth are best," said Poirot, somewhat sententiously.

"I know," said Mrs Lacey. "It's tiresome, isn't it? I mustn't be tiresome. But all the same I don't want Sarah, who's a dear girl really, to marry Desmond Lee-Wortley. She and David Welwyn, who is staying here, were always such friends and so fond of each other, and we did hope, Horace and I, that they would grow up and marry. But of course she just finds him dull now, and she's absolutely infatuated with Desmond."

"I do not quite understand, Madame," said Poirot. "You have him here now, staying in the house, this Desmond Lee-Wortley?"

"That's my doing," said Mrs Lacey. "Horace was all for forbidding her to see him and all that. Of course, in Horace's day, the father or guardian would have called round at the young man's lodgings with a horse whip! Horace was all for forbidding the fellow the house, and forbidding the girl to see him. I told him that was quite the wrong attitude to take. "No," I said. "Ask him down here. We'll have him down for Christmas with the family party." Of course, my husband said I was mad! But I said, "At any rate, dear, let's try it. Let her see him in our atmosphere and our house and we'll be very nice to him and very polite, and perhaps then he'll seem less interesting to her"!"

"I think, as they say, you have something there, Madame," said Poirot. "I think your point of view is very wise. Wiser than your husband's."

"Well, I hope it is," said Mrs Lacey doubtfully. "It doesn't seem to be working much yet. But of course he's only been here a couple of days." A sudden dimple showed in her wrinkled cheek. "I'll confess something to you, M. Poirot. I myself can't help liking him. I don't mean I really like him, with my mind, but I can feel the charm all right. Oh yes, I can see what Sarah sees in him. But I'm an old enough woman and have enough experience to know that he's absolutely no good. Even if I do enjoy his company. Though I do think," added Mrs Lacey, rather wistfully, "he has some good points. He asked if he might bring his sister here, you know. She's had an operation and was in hospital. He said it was so sad for her being in a nursing home over Christmas and he wondered if it would be too much trouble if he could bring her with him. He said he'd take all her meals up to her and all that. Well now, I do think that was rather nice of him, don't you, M. Poirot?"

"It shows a consideration," said Poirot, thoughtfully, "which seems almost out of character."

"Oh, I don't know. You can have family affections at the same time as wishing to prey on a rich young girl. Sarah will be very rich, you know, not only with what we leave her–and of course that won't be very much because most of the money goes with the place to Colin, my grandson. But her mother was a very rich woman and Sarah will inherit all her money when she's twenty-one. She's only twenty now. No, I do think it was nice of Desmond to mind about his sister. And he didn't pretend she was anything very wonderful or that. She's a shorthand typist, I gather–does secretarial work in London. And he's been as good as his word and does carry up trays to her. Not all the time, of course, but quite often. So I think he has some nice points. But all the same," said Mrs Lacey with great decision, "I don"t want Sarah to marry him."

"From all I have heard and been told," said Poirot, "that would indeed be a disaster."

"Do you think it would be possible for you to help us in any way?" asked Mrs Lacey.

"I think it is possible, yes," said Hercule Poirot, "but I do not wish to promise too much. For the Mr Desmond Lee-Wortleys of this world are clever, Madame. But do not despair. One can, perhaps, do a little something. I shall at any rate put forth my best endeavours, if only in gratitude for your kindness in asking me here for this Christmas festivity."

He looked round him. "And it cannot be so easy these days to have Christmas festivities."

"No, indeed," Mrs Lacey sighed. She leaned forward. "Do you know, M. Poirot, what I really dream of–what I would love to have?"

"But tell me, Madame."

"I simply long to have a small, modern bungalow. No, perhaps not a bungalow exactly, but a small, modern, easy to run house built somewhere in the park here, and live in it with an absolute up-to-date kitchen and no long passages. Everything easy and simple."

"It is a very practical idea, Madame."

"It"s not practical for me," said Mrs Lacey. "My husband adores this place. He loves living here. He doesn't mind being slightly uncomfortable, he doesn't mind the inconveniences and he would hate, simply hate, to live in a small modern house in the park!"

"So you sacrifice yourself to his wishes?"

Mrs Lacey drew herself up. "I do not consider it a sacrifice, M. Poirot," she said. "I married my husband with the wish to make him happy. He has been a good husband to me and made me very happy all these years, and I wish to give happiness to him."

"So you will continue to live here," said Poirot.

"It's not really too uncomfortable," said Mrs Lacey.

"No, no," said Poirot, hastily. "On the contrary, it is most comfortable. Your central heating and your bath water are perfection."

"We spent a lot of money on making the house comfortable to live in," said Mrs Lacey. "We were able to sell some land. Ripe for development, I think they call it. Fortunately right out of sight of the house on the other side of the park. Really rather an ugly bit of ground with no nice view, but we got a very good price for it. So that we have been able to have as many improvements as possible."

"But the service, Madame?"

"Oh, well, that presents less difficulty than you might think. Of course, one cannot expect to be looked after and waited upon as one used to be. Different people come in from the village. Two women in the morning, another two to cook lunch and wash it up, and different ones again in the evening. There are plenty of people who want to come and work for a few hours a day. Of course for Christmas we are very lucky. My dear Mrs Ross always comes in every Christmas. She is a wonderful cook, really firstclass. She retired about ten years ago, but she comes in to help us in any emergency. Then there is dear Peverell."

"Your butler?"

"Yes. He is pensioned off and lives in the little house near the lodge, but he is so devoted, and he insists on coming to wait on us at Christmas. Really, I'm terrified, M. Poirot, because he's so old and so shaky that I feel certain that if he carries anything heavy he will drop it. It's really an agony to watch him. And his heart is not good and I'm afraid of his doing too much. But it would hurt his feelings dreadfully if I did not let him come. He hems and hahs and makes disapproving noises when he sees the state our silver is in and within three days of being here, it is all wonderful again. Yes. He is a dear faithful friend." She smiled at Poirot. "So you see, we are all set for a happy Christmas. A white Christmas, too," she added as she looked out of the window. "See? It is beginning to snow. Ah, the children are coming in. You must meet them, M. Poirot."

Poirot was introduced with due ceremony. First, to Colin and Michael, the schoolboy grandson and his friend, nice polite lads of fifteen, one dark, one fair. Then to their cousin, Bridget, a black-haired girl of about the same age with enormous vitality.

"And this is my granddaughter, Sarah," said Mrs Lacey.

Poirot looked with some interest at Sarah, an attractive girl with a mop of red hair; her manner seemed to him nervy and a trifle defiant, but she showed real affection for her grandmother.

"And this is Mr Lee-Wortley."

Mr Lee-Wortley wore a fisherman's jersey and tight black jeans; his hair was rather long and it seemed doubtful whether he had shaved that morning. In contrast to him was a young man introduced as David Welwyn, who was solid and quiet, with a pleasant smile, and rather obviously addicted to soap and water. There was one other member of the party, a handsome, rather intense-looking girl who was introduced as Diana Middleton.

Tea was brought in. A hearty meal of scones, crumpets, sandwiches and three kinds of cake. The younger members of the party appreciated the tea. Colonel Lacey came in last, remarking in a noncommittal voice: "Hey, tea? Oh yes, tea."

He received his cup of tea from his wife's hand, helped himself to two scones, cast a look of aversion at Desmond Lee-Wortley and sat down as far away from him as he could. He was a big man with bushy eyebrows and a red, weather-beaten face. He might have been taken for a farmer rather than the lord of the manor.

"Started to snow," he said. "It's going to be a white Christmas all right."

After tea the party dispersed.

"I expect they'll go and play with their tape recorders now," said Mrs Lacey to Poirot. She looked indulgently after her grandson as he left the room. Her tone was that of one who says "The children are going to play with their toy soldiers."

"They're frightfully technical, of course," she said, "and very grand about it all."

The boys and Bridget, however, decided to go along to the lake and see if the ice on it was likely to make skating possible.

"I thought we could have skated on it this morning," said Colin. "But old Hodgkins said no. He"s always so terribly careful."

"Come for a walk, David," said Diana Middleton, softly.

David hesitated for half a moment, his eyes on Sarah's red head. She was standing by Desmond Lee-Wortley, her hand on his arm, looking up into his face.

"All right," said David Welwyn, "yes, let's."

Diana slipped a quick hand through his arm and they turned towards the door into the garden. Sarah said:

"Shall we go, too, Desmond? It's fearfully stuffy in the house."

"Who wants to walk?" said Desmond. "I'll get my car out. We'll go along to the Speckled Boar and have a drink."

Sarah hesitated for a moment before saying:

"Let's go to Market Ledbury to the White Hart. It's much more fun."

Though for all the world she would not have put it into words, Sarah had an instinctive revulsion from going down to the local pub with Desmond. It was, somehow, not in the tradition of Kings Lacey. The women of Kings Lacey had never frequented the bar of the Speckled Boar. She had an obscure feeling that to go there would be to let old Colonel Lacey and his wife down. And why not? Desmond Lee-Wortley would have said. For a moment of exasperation Sarah felt that he ought to know why not! One didn't upset such old darlings as Grandfather and dear old Em unless it was necessary. They'd been very sweet, really, letting her lead her own life, not understanding in the least why she wanted to live in Chelsea in the way she did, but accepting it. That was due to Em of course. Grandfather would have kicked up no end of a row.

Sarah had no illusions about her grandfather's attitude. It was not his doing that Desmond had been asked to stay at Kings Lacey. That was Em, and Em was a darling and always had been.

When Desmond had gone to fetch his car, Sarah popped her head into the drawing-room again.

"We're going over to Market Ledbury," she said. "We thought we'd have a drink there at the White Hart."

There was a slight amount of defiance in her voice, but Mrs Lacey did not seem to notice it.

"Well, dear," she said. "I'm sure that will be very nice. David and Diana have gone for a walk, I see. I'm so glad. I really think it was a brainwave on my part to ask Diana here. So sad being left a widow so young–only twenty-two–I do hope she marries again soon."

Sarah looked at her sharply. "What are you up to, Em?"

"It's my little plan," said Mrs Lacey gleefully. "I think she's just right for David. Of course I know he was terribly in love with you, Sarah dear, but you'd no use for him and I realize that he isn't your type. But I don't want him to go on being unhappy, and I think Diana will really suit him."

"What a matchmaker you are, Em," said Sarah. "I know," said Mrs Lacey.

"Old women always are. Diana's quite keen on him already, I think. Don't you think she'd be just right for him?"

"I shouldn't say so," said Sarah. "I think Diana's far too–well, too intense, too serious. I should think David would find it terribly boring being married to her."

"Well, we'll see," said Mrs Lacey. "Anyway, you don't want him, do you, dear?"

"No, indeed," said Sarah, very quickly. She added, in a sudden rush, "Youdo like Desmond, don't you, Em?"

"I'm sure he's very nice indeed," said Mrs Lacey.

"Grandfather doesn't like him," said Sarah.

"Well, you could hardly expect him to, could you?" said Mrs Lacey reasonably, "but I dare say he'll come round when he gets used to the idea. You mustn't rush him, Sarah dear. Old people are very slow to change their minds and your grandfather is rather obstinate."

"I don't care what Grandfather thinks or says," said Sarah. "I shall get married to Desmond whenever I like!"

"I know, dear, I know. But do try and be realistic about it. Your grandfather could cause a lot of trouble, you know. You're not of age yet. In another year you can do as you please. I expect Horace will have come round long before that."

"You're on my side aren't you, darling?" said Sarah. She flung her arms round her grandmother's neck and gave her an affectionate kiss.

"I want you to be happy," said Mrs Lacey. "Ah! there's your young man bringing his car round. You know, I like these very tight trousers these young men wear nowadays. They look so smart–only, of course, it does accentuate knock knees."

Yes, Sarah thought, Desmond had got knock knees, she had never noticed it before . . .

"Go on, dear, enjoy yourself," said Mrs Lacey.

She watched her go out to the car, then, remembering her foreign guest, she went along to the library. Looking in, however, she saw that Hercule Poirot was taking a pleasant little nap and, smiling to herself, she went across the hall and out into the kitchen to have a conference with Mrs Ross.

"Come on, beautiful," said Desmond. "Your family cutting up rough because you're coming out to a pub? Years behind the times here, aren't they?"

"Of course they're not making a fuss," said Sarah, sharply as she got into the car.

"What's the idea of having that foreign fellow down? He's a detective, isn't he? What needs detecting here?"

"Oh, he's not here professionally," said Sarah. "Edwina Morecombe, my grandmother, asked us to have him. I think he's retired from professional work long ago."

"Sounds like a broken-down old cab horse," said Desmond.

"He wanted to see an old-fashioned English Christmas, I believe," said Sarah vaguely.

Desmond laughed scornfully. "Such a lot of tripe, that sort of thing," he said. "How you can stand it I don't know."

Sarah's red hair was tossed back and her aggressive chin shot up.

"I enjoy it!" she said defiantly.

"You can't, baby. Let's cut the whole thing tomorrow. Go over to Scarborough or somewhere."

"I couldn't possibly do that."

"Why not?"

"Oh, it would hurt their feelings."

"Oh, bilge! You know you don't enjoy this childish sentimental bosh."

"Well, not really perhaps, but–" Sarah broke off. She realized with a feeling of guilt that she was looking forward a good deal to the Christmas celebration. She enjoyed the whole thing, but she was ashamed to admit that to Desmond. It was not the thing to enjoy Christmas and family life. Just for a moment she wished that Desmond had not come down here at Christmas time. In fact, she almost wished that Desmond had not come down here at all. It was much more fun seeing Desmond in London than here at home.

In the meantime the boys and Bridget were walking back from the lake, still discussing earnestly the problems of skating. Flecks of snow had been falling, and looking up at the sky it could be prophesied that before long there was going to be a heavy snowfall.

"It's going to snow all night," said Colin. "Bet you by Christmas morning we have a couple of feet of snow."

The prospect was a pleasurable one.

"Let's make a snowman," said Michael. "Good lord," said Colin, "I haven't made a snowman since–well, since I was about four years old."

"I don't believe it's a bit easy to do," said Bridget. "I mean, you have to know how."

"We might make an effigy of M. Poirot," said Colin. "Give it a big black moustache. There is one in the dressing-up box."

"I don't see, you know," said Michael thoughtfully, "how M. Poirot could ever have been a detective. I don't see how he'd ever be able to disguise himself."

"I know," said Bridget, "and one can't imagine him running about with a microscope and looking for clues or measuring footprints."

"I've got an idea," said Colin. "Let's put on a show for him!"

"What do you mean, a show?" asked Bridget.

"Well, arrange a murder for him."

"What a gorgeous idea," said Bridget. "Do you mean a body in the snow–that sort of thing?"

"Yes. It would make him feel at home, wouldn't it?"

Bridget giggled.

"I don't know that I'd go as far as that."

"If it snows," said Colin, "we'll have the perfect setting. A body and footprints–we'll have to think that out rather carefully and pinch one of Grandfather's daggers and make some blood."

They came to a halt and, oblivious to the rapidly falling snow, entered into an excited discussion.

"There's a paintbox in the old schoolroom. We could mix up some blood–crimson-lake, I should think."

"Crimson-lake's a bit too pink, I think," said Bridget. "It ought to be a bit browner."

"Who's going to be the body?" asked Michael.

"I'll be the body," said Bridget quickly.

"Oh, look here," said Colin, "I thought of it."

"Oh, no, no," said Bridget, "it must be me. It"s got to be a girl. It's more exciting. Beautiful girl lying lifeless in the snow."

"Beautiful girl! Ah-ha," said Michael in derision.

"I've got black hair, too," said Bridget.

"What's that got to do with it?"

"Well, it'll show up so well on the snow and I shall wear my red pyjamas."

"If you wear red pyjamas, they won't show the bloodstains," said Michael in a practical manner.

"But they'd look so effective against the snow," said Bridget, "and they've got white facings, you know, so the blood could be on that. Oh, won't it be gorgeous? Do you think he will really be taken in?"

"He will if we do it well enough," said Michael. "We'll have just your footprints in the snow and one other person's going to the body and coming away from it–a man's, of course. He won't want to disturb them, so he won't know that you're not really dead. You don't think," Michael stopped, struck by a sudden idea. The others looked at him. "You don't think he'll be annoyed about it?"

"Oh, I shouldn't think so," said Bridget, with facile optimism. "I'm sure he'll understand that we've just done it to entertain him. A sort of Christmas treat."

"I don't think we ought to do it on Christmas Day," said Colin reflectively. "I don't think Grandfather would like that very much."

"Boxing Day then," said Bridget.

"Boxing Day would be just right," said Michael.

"And it'll give us more time, too," pursued Bridget. "After all, there are a lot of things to arrange. Let's go and have a look at all the props."

They hurried into the house.

III

The evening was a busy one. Holly and mistletoe had been brought in in large quantities and a Christmas tree had been set up at one end of the dining-room. Everyone helped to decorate it, to put up the branches of holly behind pictures and to hang mistletoe in a convenient position in the hall.

"I had no idea anything so archaic still went on," murmured Desmond to Sarah with a sneer.

"We've always done it," said Sarah, defensively.

"What a reason!"

"Oh, don't be tiresome, Desmond. I think it's fun."

"Sarah my sweet, you can't!"

"Well, not–not really perhaps but–I do in a way."

"Who's going to brave the snow and go to midnight mass?" asked Mrs Lacey at twenty minutes to twelve.

"Not me," said Desmond. "Come on, Sarah."

With a hand on her arm he guided her into the library and went over to the record case.

"There are limits, darling," said Desmond. "Midnight mass!"

"Yes," said Sarah. "Oh yes."

With a good deal of laughter, donning of coats and stamping of feet, most of the others got off. The two boys, Bridget, David and Diana set out for the ten minutes' walk to the church through the falling snow. Their laughter died away in the distance.

"Midnight mass!" said Colonel Lacey, snorting. "Never went to midnight mass in my young days. Mass, indeed! Popish, that is! Oh, I beg your pardon, M. Poirot."

Poirot waved a hand. "It is quite all right. Do not mind me."

"Matins is good enough for anybody, I should say," said the colonel.

"Proper Sunday morning service. "Hark the herald angels sing," and all the good old Christmas hymns. And then back to Christmas dinner. That's right, isn't it, Em?"

"Yes, dear," said Mrs Lacey. "That's what we do. But the young ones enjoy the midnight service. And it's nice, really, that they want to go."

"Sarah and that fellow don't want to go."

"Well, there dear, I think you're wrong," said Mrs Lacey. "Sarah, you know, did want to go, but she didn't like to say so."

"Beats me why she cares what that fellow's opinion is."

"She's very young, really," said Mrs Lacey placidly. "Are you going to bed, M. Poirot? Good night. I hope you'll sleep well."

"And you, Madame? Are you not going to bed yet?"

"Not just yet," said Mrs Lacey. "I've got the stockings to fill, you see. Oh, I know they're all practically grown up, but they do like their stockings. One puts jokes in them! Silly little things. But it all makes for a lot of fun."

"You work very hard to make this a happy house at Christmas time," said Poirot. "I honour you."

He raised her hand to his lips in a courtly fashion.

"Hm," grunted Colonel Lacey, as Poirot departed. "Flowery sort of fellow. Still–he appreciates you."

Mrs Lacey dimpled up at him. "Have you noticed, Horace, that I'm standing under the mistletoe?" she asked with the demureness of a girl of nineteen.

Hercule Poirot entered his bedroom. It was a large room well provided with radiators. As he went over towards the big four-poster bed he noticed an envelope lying on his pillow. He opened it and drew out a piece of paper. On it was a shakily printed message in capital letters.

DON'T EAT NONE OF THE PLUM PUDDING. ONE AS WISHES YOU WELL.

Hercule Poirot stared at it. His eyebrows rose. "Cryptic," he murmured, "and most unexpected."

IV

Christmas dinner took place at 2 p.m. and was a feast indeed. Enormous logs crackled merrily in the wide fireplace and above their crackling rose the babel of many tongues talking together. Oyster soup had been consumed, two enormous turkeys had come and gone, mere carcasses of their former selves. Now, the supreme moment, the Christmas pudding was brought in, in state! Old Peverell, his hands and his knees shaking with the weakness of eighty years, permitted no one but himself to bear it in. Mrs Lacey sat, her hands pressed together in nervous apprehension. One Christmas, she felt sure, Peverell would fall down dead. Having either to take the risk of letting him fall down dead or of hurting his feelings to such an extent that he would probably prefer to be dead than alive, she had so far chosen the former alternative. On a silver dish the Christmas pudding reposed in its glory. A large football of a pudding, a piece of holly stuck in it like a triumphant flag and glorious flames of blue and red rising round it. There was a cheer and cries of "Ooh-ah."

One thing Mrs Lacey had done: prevailed upon Peverell to place the pudding in front of her so that she could help it rather than hand it in turn round the table. She breathed a sigh of relief as it was deposited safely in front of her. Rapidly the plates were passed round, flames still licking the portions.

"Wish, M. Poirot," cried Bridget. "Wish before the flame goes. Quick, Gran darling, quick."

Mrs Lacey leant back with a sigh of satisfaction. Operation Pudding had been a success. In front of everyone was a helping with flames still licking it. There was a momentary silence all round the table as everyone wished hard.

There was nobody to notice the rather curious expression on the face of M.Poirot as he surveyed the portion of pudding on his plate. "Don't eat none of the plum pudding." What on earth did that sinister warning mean? There could be nothing different about his portion of plum pudding from that of everyone else! Sighing as he admitted himself baffled–and Hercule Poirot never liked to admit himself baffled–he picked up his spoon and fork.

"Hard sauce, M. Poirot?"

Poirot helped himself appreciatively to hard sauce. "Swiped my best brandy again, eh Em?" said the colonel good-humouredly from the other end of the table. Mrs Lacey twinkled at him.

"Mrs Ross insists on having the best brandy, dear," she said. "She says it makes all the difference."

"Well, well," said Colonel Lacey, "Christmas comes but once a year and Mrs Ross is a great woman. A great woman and a great cook."

"She is indeed," said Colin. "Smashing plum pudding, this. Mmmm." He filled an appreciative mouth.

Gently, almost gingerly, Hercule Poirot attacked his portion of pudding. He ate a mouthful. It was delicious! He ate another. Something tinkled faintly on his plate. He investigated with a fork. Bridget, on his left, came to his aid.

"You've got something, M. Poirot," she said. "I wonder what it is"

Poirot detached a little silver object from the surrounding raisins that clung to it.

"Oooh," said Bridget, "it's the bachelor's button! M. Poirot's got the bachelor's button!"

Hercule Poirot dipped the small silver button into the finger-glass of water that stood by his plate, and washed it clear of pudding crumbs.

"It is very pretty," he observed. "That means you're going to be a bachelor, M. Poirot," explained Colin helpfully.

"That is to be expected," said Poirot gravely. "I have been a bachelor for many long years and it is unlikely that I shall change that status now."

"Oh, never say die," said Michael. "I saw in the paper that someone of ninety-five married a girl of twenty-two the other day."

"You encourage me," said Hercule Poirot.

Colonel Lacey uttered a sudden exclamation. His face became purple and his hand went to his mouth.

"Confound it, Emmeline," he roared, "why on earth do you let the cook put glass in the pudding?"

"Glass!" cried Mrs Lacey, astonished.

Colonel Lacey withdrew the offending substance from his mouth. "Might have broken a tooth," he grumbled. "Or swallowed the damn" thing and had appendicitis."

He dropped the piece of glass into the finger-bowl, rinsed it and held it up.

"God bless my soul," he ejaculated. "It's a red stone out of one of the cracker brooches." He held it aloft.

"You permit?"

Very deftly M. Poirot stretched across his neighbour, took it from Colonel Lacey's fingers and examined it attentively. As the squire had said, it was an enormous red stone the colour of a ruby. The light gleamed from its facets as he turned it about. Somewhere around the table a chair was pushed sharply back and then drawn in again.

"Phew!" cried Michael. "How wizard it would be if it was real."

"Perhaps it is real," said Bridget hopefully.

"Oh, don't be an ass, Bridget. Why a ruby of that size would be worth thousands and thousands and thousands of pounds. Wouldn't it, M. Poirot?"

"It would indeed," said Poirot. "But what I can't understand," said Mrs Lacey, "is how it got into the pudding."

"Oooh," said Colin, diverted by his last mouthful, "I've got the pig. It isn't fair."

Bridget chanted immediately, "Colin's got the pig! Colin's got the pig! Colin is the greedy guzzling pig!"

"I've got the ring," said Diana in a clear, high voice.

"Good for you, Diana. You'll be married first, of us all."

"I've got the thimble," wailed Bridget.

"Bridget's going to be an old maid," chanted the two boys. "Yah, Bridget's going to be an old maid."

"Who's got the money?" demanded David. "There's a real ten-shilling piece, gold, in this pudding. I know. Mrs Ross told me so."

"I think I'm the lucky one," said Desmond Lee-Wortley.

Colonel Lacey's two next-door neighbours heard him mutter, "Yes, you would be."

"I've got a ring, too," said David. He looked across at Diana. "Quite a coincidence, isn't it?"

The laughter went on. Nobody noticed that M. Poirot carelessly, as though thinking of something else, had dropped the red stone into his pocket.

Mince-pies and Christmas dessert followed the pudding. The older members of the party then retired for a welcome siesta before the tea-time ceremony of the lighting of the Christmas tree. Hercule Poirot, however, did not take a siesta. Instead, he made his way to the enormous old-fashioned kitchen.

"It is permitted," he asked, looking round and beaming, "that I congratulate the cook on this marvellous meal that I have just eaten?"

There was a moment's pause and then Mrs Ross came forward in a stately manner to meet him. She was a large woman, nobly built with all the dignity of a stage duchess. Two lean grey-haired women were beyond in the scullery washing up and a tow-haired girl was moving to and fro between the scullery and the kitchen. But these were obviously mere myrmidons. Mrs Ross was the queen of the kitchen quarters.

"I am glad to hear you enjoyed it, sir," she said graciously.

"Enjoyed it!" cried Hercule Poirot. With an extravagant foreign gesture he raised his hand to his lips, kissed it, and wafted the kiss to the ceiling. "But you are a genius, Mrs

Ross! A genius! Never have I tasted such a wonderful meal. The oyster soup–" he made an expressive noise with his lips"–and the stuffing. The chestnut stuffing in the turkey, that was quite unique in my experience."

"Well, it's funny that you should say that, sir," said Mrs Ross graciously. "It's a very special recipe, that stuffing. It was given me by an Austrian chef that I worked with many years ago. But all the rest," she added, "is just good, plain English cooking."

"And is there anything better?" demanded Hercule Poirot.

"Well, it's nice of you to say so, sir. Of course, you being a foreign gentleman might have preferred the continental style. Not but what I can't manage continental dishes too."

"I am sure, Mrs Ross, you could manage anything! But you must know that English cooking–good English cooking, not the cooking one gets in the second-class hotels or the restaurants–is much appreciated by gourmets on the continent, and I believe I am correct in saying that a special expedition was made to London in the early eighteen hundreds, and a report sent back to France of the wonders of the English puddings. "We have nothing like that in France," they wrote. "It is worth making a journey to London just to taste the varieties and excellencies of the English puddings." And above all puddings," continued Poirot, well launched now on a kind of rhapsody, "is the Christmas plum pudding, such as we have eaten today. That was a home-made pudding, was it not? Not a bought one?"

"Yes, indeed, sir. Of my own making and my own recipe such as I've made for many years. When I came here Mrs Lacey said that she'd ordered a pudding from a London store to save me the trouble. But no, Madam, I said, that may be kind of you but no bought pudding from a store can equal a home-made Christmas one. Mind you," said Mrs Ross, warming to her subject like the artist she was, "it was made too soon before the day. A good Christmas pudding should be made some weeks before and allowed to wait. The longer they're kept, within reason, the better they are. I mind now that when I was a child and we went to church every Sunday, we'd start listening for the collect that begins "Stir up O Lord we beseech thee" because that collect was the signal, as it were, that the puddings should be made that week. And so they always were. We had the collect on the Sunday, and that week sure enough my mother would make the Christmas puddings. And so it should have been here this year. As it was, that pudding was only made three days ago, the day before you arrived, sir. However, I kept to the old custom. Everyone in the house had to come out into the kitchen and have a stir and make a wish. That's an old custom, sir, and I've always held to it."

"Most interesting," said Hercule Poirot. "Most interesting. And so everyone came out into the kitchen?"

"Yes, sir. The young gentlemen, Miss Bridget and the London gentleman who's staying here, and his sister and Mr David and Miss Diana—Mrs Middleton, I should say—All had a stir, they did."

"How many puddings did you make? Is this the only one?"

"No, sir, I made four. Two large ones and two smaller ones. The other large one I planned to serve on New Year's Day and the smaller ones were for Colonel and Mrs Lacey when they're alone like and not so many in the family."

"I see, I see," said Poirot.

"As a matter of fact, sir," said Mrs Ross, "it was the wrong pudding you had for lunch today."

"The wrong pudding?" Poirot frowned. "How is that?"

"Well, sir, we have a big Christmas mould. A china mould with a pattern of holly and mistletoe on top and we always have the Christmas Day pudding boiled in that. But there was a most unfortunate accident. This morning, when Annie was getting it down from the shelf in the larder, she slipped and dropped it and it broke. Well, sir, naturally I couldn't serve that, could I? There might have been splinters in it. So we had to use the other one–the New Year"s Day one, which was in a plain bowl. It makes a nice round but it's not so decorative as the Christmas mould. Really, where we'll get another mould like that I don't know. They don't make things in that size nowadays. All tiddly bits of things. Why, you can't even buy a breakfast dish that'll take a proper eight to ten eggs and bacon. Ah, things aren't what they were."

"No, indeed," said Poirot. "But today that is not so. This Christmas Day has been like the Christmas Days of old, is that not true?"

Mrs Ross sighed. "Well, I'm glad you say so, sir, but of course I haven't the help now that I used to have. Not skilled help, that is. The girls nowadays–" she lowered her voice slightly,"– they mean very well and they're very willing but they've not been trained, sir, if you understand what I mean."

"Times change, yes," said Hercule Poirot. "I too find it sad sometimes."

"This house, sir," said Mrs Ross, "it's too large, you know, for the mistress and the colonel. The mistress, she knows that. Living in a corner of it as they do, it's not the same thing at all. It only comes alive, as you might say, at Christmas time when all the family come."

"It is the first time, I think, that Mr Lee-Wortley and his sister have been here?"

"Yes, sir." A note of slight reserve crept into Mrs Ross's voice. "A very nice gentleman he is but, well–it seems a funny friend for Miss Sarah to have, according to our ideas. But there–London ways are different! It's sad that his sister's so poorly. Had an operation, she had. She seemed all right the first day she was here, but that very day, after we'd been stirring the puddings, she was took bad again and she's been in bed ever since. Got up too soon after her operation, I expect. Ah, doctors nowadays, they have you out of hospital before you can hardly stand on your feet. Why, my very own nephew's wife . . ." And Mrs Ross went into a long and spirited tale of hospital treatment as accorded to her relations, comparing it unfavourably with the consideration that had been lavished upon them in older times.

Poirot duly commiserated with her. "It remains," he said, "to thank you for this exquisite and sumptuous meal. You permit a little acknowledgement of my appreciation?" A crisp five-pound note passed from his hand into that of Mrs Ross who said perfunctorily:

"You really shouldn't do that, sir."

"I insist. I insist."

"Well, it's very kind of you indeed, sir." Mrs Ross accepted the tribute as no more than her due. "And I wish you, sir, a very happy Christmas and a prosperous New Year."

V

The end of Christmas Day was like the end of most Christmas Days. The tree was lighted, a splendid Christmas cake came in for tea, was greeted with approval but was partaken of only moderately. There was cold supper. Both Poirot and his host and hostess went to bed early.

"Good night, M. Poirot," said Mrs Lacey. "I hope you've enjoyed yourself."

"It has been a wonderful day, Madame, wonderful."

"You're looking very thoughtful," said Mrs Lacey.

"It is the English pudding that I consider."

"You found it a little heavy, perhaps?" asked Mrs Lacey delicately.

"No, no, I do not speak gastronomically. I consider its significance."

"It's traditional, of course," said Mrs Lacey. "Well, good night, M. Poirot, and don't dream too much of Christmas puddings and mince-pies."

"Yes," murmured Poirot to himself as he undressed. "It is a problem certainly, that Christmas plum pudding. There is here something that I do not understand at all." He shook his head in a vexed manner. "Well–we shall see."

After making certain preparations, Poirot went to bed, but not to sleep. It was some two hours later that his patience was rewarded. The door of his bedroom opened very gently. He smiled to himself. It was as he had thought it would be. His mind went back fleetingly to the cup of coffee so politely handed him by Desmond Lee-Wortley. A little later, when Desmond's back was turned, he had laid the cup down for a few moments on a table. He had then apparently picked it up again and Desmond had had the satisfaction, if satisfaction it was, of seeing him drink the coffee to the last drop. But a little smile lifted Poirot's moustache as hc reflected that it was not he but someone else who was sleeping a good sound sleep tonight.

"That pleasant young David," said Poirot to himself, "he is worried, unhappy. It will do him no harm to have a night's really sound sleep. And now, let us see what will happen?"

He lay quite still, breathing in an even manner with occasionally a suggestion, but the very faintest suggestion, of a snore. Someone came up to the bed and bent over him. Then, satisfied, that someone turned away and went to the dressing-table. By the light of a tiny torch the visitor was examining Poirot"s belongings neatly arranged on top of the dressing-table. Fingers explored the wallet, gently pulled open the drawers of the dressing-table, then extended the search to the pockets of Poirot's clothes. Finally the visitor approached the bed and with great caution slid his hand under the pillow. Withdrawing his hand, he stood for a moment or two as though uncertain what to do next. He walked round the room looking inside ornaments, went into the adjoining bathroom from whence he presently returned. Then, with a faint exclamation of disgust, he went out of the room.

"Ah," said Poirot, under his breath. "You have a disappointment. Yes, yes, a serious disappointment. Bah! To imagine, even, that Hercule Poirot would hide something where you could find it!" Then, turning over on his other side, he went peacefully to sleep.

He was aroused next morning by an urgent soft tapping on his door.

"Qui est là? Come in, come in."

The door opened. Breathless, red-faced, Colin stood upon the threshold. Behind him stood Michael.

"Monsieur Poirot, Monsieur Poirot."

"But yes?" Poirot sat up in bed. "It is the early tea? But no. It is you, Colin. What has occurred?"

Colin was, for a moment, speechless. He seemed to be under the grip of some strong emotion. In actual fact it was the sight of the nightcap that Hercule Poirot wore that affected for the moment his organs of speech. Presently he controlled himself and spoke.

"I think–M. Poirot, could you help us? Something rather awful has happened."

"Something has happened? But what?"

"It's–it's Bridget. She's out there in the snow. I think–she doesn't move or speak and–oh, you'd better come and look for yourself. I'm terribly afraid–she may be dead."

"What?" Poirot cast aside his bed covers. "Mademoiselle Bridget–dead!"

"I think–I think somebody's killed her. There's–there's blood and–oh do come!"

"But certainly. But certainly. I come on the instant."

With great practicality Poirot inserted his feet into his outdoor shoes and pulled a fur-lined overcoat over his pyjamas.

"I come," he said. "I come on the moment. You have aroused the house?"

"No. No, so far I haven't told anyone but you. I thought it would be better. Grandfather and Gran aren't up yet. They're laying breakfast downstairs, but I didn't say anything to Peverell. She–Bridget–she's round the other side of the house, near the terrace and the library window."

"I see. Lead the way. I will follow."

Turning away to hide his delighted grin, Colin led the way downstairs. They went out through the side door. It was a clear morning with the sun not yet high over the horizon. It was not snowing now, but it had snowed heavily during the night and everywhere around was an unbroken carpet of thick snow. The world looked very pure and white and beautiful.

"There!" said Colin breathlessly. "I–it's–there!" He pointed dramatically.

The scene was indeed dramatic enough. A few yards away Bridget lay in the snow. She was wearing scarlet pyjamas and a white wool wrap thrown round her shoulders. The white wool wrap was stained with crimson. Her head was turned aside and hidden by the mass of her outspread black hair. One arm was under her body, the other lay flung out, the fingers clenched, and standing up in the centre of the crimson stain was the hilt of a large curved Kurdish knife which Colonel Lacey had shown to his guests only the evening before.

"Mon Dieu! " ejaculated M. Poirot. "It is like something on the stage!"

There was a faint choking noise from Michael. Colin thrust himself quickly into the breach.

"I know," he said. "It–it doesn't seem real somehow, does it. Do you see those footprints–I suppose we mustn't disturb them?"

"Ah yes, the footprints. No, we must be careful not to disturb those footprints."

"That's what I thought," said Colin. "That's why I wouldn't let anyone go near her until we got you. I thought you'd know what to do."

"All the same," said Hercule Poirot briskly, "first, we must see if she is still alive? Is not that so?"

"Well–yes–of course," said Michael, a little doubtfully. "but you see, we thought–I mean, we didn't like–"

"Ah, you have the prudence! You have read the detective stories. It is most important that nothing should be touched and that the body should be left as it is. But we cannot be sure as yet if it is a body, can we? After all, though prudence is admirable, common humanity comes first. We must think of the doctor, must we not, before we think of the police?"

"Oh yes. Of course," said Colin, still a little taken aback.

"We only thought–I mean–we thought we'd better get you before we did anything," said Michael hastily.

"Then you will both remain here," said Poirot. "I will approach from the other side so as not to disturb these footprints. Such excellent footprints, are they not–so very clear? The footprints of a man and a girl going out together to the place where she lies. And then the man's footsteps come back but the girl's–do not."

"They must be the footprints of the murderer," said Colin, with bated breath.

"Exactly," said Poirot. "The footprints of the murderer. A long narrow foot with rather a peculiar type of shoe. Very interesting. Easy, I think, to recognize. Yes, those footprints will be very important."

At that moment Desmond Lee-Wortley came out of the house with Sarah and joined them.

"What on earth are you all doing here?" he demanded in a somewhat theatrical manner. "I saw you from my bedroom window. What"s up? Good lord, what's this? It–it looks like–"

"Exactly," said Hercule Poirot. "It looks like murder, does it not?"

Sarah gave a gasp, then shot a quick suspicious glance at the two boys.

"You mean someone's killed the girl–what's-her-name–Bridget?" demanded Desmond. "Who on earth would want to kill her? It's unbelievable!"

"There are many things that are unbelievable," said Poirot. "Especially before breakfast, is it not? That is what one of your classics says. Six impossible things before breakfast." He added: "Please wait here, all of you."

Carefully making a circuit, he approached Bridget and bent for a moment down over the body. Colin and Michael were now both shaking with suppressed laughter. Sarah joined them, murmuring "What have you two been up to?"

"Good old Bridget," whispered Colin. "Isn't she wonderful? Not a twitch!"

"I've never seen anything look so dead as Bridget does," whispered Michael.

Hercule Poirot straightened up again.

"This is a terrible thing," he said. His voice held an emotion it had not held before.

Overcome by mirth, Michael and Colin both turned away. In a choked voice Michael said:

"What–what must we do?"

"There is only one thing to do," said Poirot. "We must send for the police. Will one of you telephone or would you prefer me to do it?"

"I think," said Colin, "I think–what about it, Michael?"

"Yes," said Michael, "I think the jig's up now." He stepped forward. For the first time he seemed a little unsure of himself. "I'm awfully sorry," he said, "I hope you won't mind too much. It–er–it was a sort of joke for Christmas and all that, you know. We thought we'd–well, lay on a murder for you."

"You thought you would lay on a murder for me? Then this– then this–"

"It's just a show we put on," explained Colin, "to–to make you feel at home, you know."

"Aha," said Hercule Poirot. "I understand. You make of me the April fool, is that it? But today is not April the first, it is December the twenty-sixth."

"I suppose we oughtn't to have done it really," said Colin, "but–but–you don't mind very much, do you, M. Poirot?

Come on, Bridget," he called, "get up. You must be half-frozen to death already."

The figure in the snow, however, did not stir. "It is odd," said Hercule Poirot, "she does not seem to hear you." He looked thoughtfully at them. "It is a joke, you say? You are sure this is a joke?"

"Why, yes." Colin spoke uncomfortably. "We–we didn't mean any harm."

"But why then does Mademoiselle Bridget not get up?"

"I can't imagine," said Colin.

"Come on, Bridget," said Sarah impatiently. "Don't go on lying there playing the fool."

"We really are very sorry, M. Poirot," said Colin apprehensively. "We do really apologize."

"You need not apologize," said Poirot, in a peculiar tone.

"What do you mean?" Colin stared at him. He turned again. "Bridget! Bridget! What's the matter? Why doesn't she get up? Why does she go on lying there?"

Poirot beckoned to Desmond. "You, Mr Lee-Wortley. Come here–"

Desmond joined him.

"Feel her pulse," said Poirot.

Desmond Lee-Wortley bent down. He touched the arm–the wrist. "There"s no pulse . . ." He stared at Poirot. "Her arm's still. Good God, she really is dead!"

Poirot nodded. "Yes, she is dead," he said. "Someone has turned the comedy into a tragedy."

"Someone–who?"

"There is a set of footprints going and returning. A set of footprints that bears a strong resemblance to the footprints you have just made, Mr Lee-Wortley, coming from the path to this spot."

Desmond Lee-Wortley wheeled round. "What on earth–Are you accusing me? ME? You're crazy! Why on earth should I want to kill the girl?"

"Ah – why? I wonder . . . Let us see . . ."

He bent down and very gently prised open the stiff fingers of the girl's clenched hand.

Desmond drew a sharp breath. He gazed down unbelievingly. In the palm of the dead girl's hand was what appeared to be a large ruby.

"It's that damn thing out of the pudding!" he cried.

"Is it?" said Poirot. "Are you sure?"

"Of course it is."

With a swift movement Desmond bent down and plucked the red stone out of Bridget's hand.

"You should not do that," said Poirot reproachfully. "Nothing should have been disturbed."

"I haven't disturbed the body, have I? But this thing might– might get lost and it's evidence. The great thing is to get the police here as soon as possible. I'll go at once and telephone."

He wheeled round and ran sharply towards the house. Sarah came swiftly to Poirot's side.

"I don't understand," she whispered. Her face was dead white. "I don't understand." She caught at Poirot's arm. "What did you mean about–about the footprints?"

"Look for yourself, Mademoiselle."

The footprints that led to the body and back again were the same as the ones just made accompanying Poirot to the girl's body and back.

"You mean–that it was Desmond? Nonsense!"

Suddenly the noise of a car came through the clear air. They wheeled round. They saw the car clearly enough driving at a furious pace down the drive and Sarah recognized what car it was.

"It's Desmond," she said. "It's Desmond"s car. He–he must have gone to fetch the police instead of telephoning."

Diana Middleton came running out of the house to join them.

"What's happened?" she cried in a breathless voice. "Desmond just came rushing into the house. He said something about Bridget being killed and then he rattled the telephone but it was dead. He couldn't get an answer. He said the wires must have been cut. He said the only thing was to take a car and go for the police. Why the police? . . ."

Poirot made a gesture.

"Bridget?" Diana stared at him. "But surely–isn't it a joke of some kind? I heard something – something last night. I thought that they were going to play a joke on you, M. Poirot?"

"Yes," said Poirot, "that was the idea–to play a joke on me. But now come into the house, all of you. We shall catch our deaths of cold here and there is nothing to be done until Mr Lee-Wortley returns with the police."

"But look here," said Colin, "we can't–we can't leave Bridget here alone."

"You can do her no good by remaining," said Poirot gently. "Come, it is a sad, a very sad tragedy, but there is nothing we can do any more to help Mademoiselle Bridget. So let us come in and get warm and have perhaps a cup of tea or of coffee."

They followed him obediently into the house. Peverell was just about to strike the gong. If he thought it extraordinary for most of the household to be outside and for Poirot to make an appearance in pyjamas and an overcoat, he displayed no sign of it. Peverell in his old age was still the perfect butler. He noticed nothing that he was not asked to notice. They went into the dining-room and sat down. When they all had a cup of coffee in front of them and were sipping it, Poirot spoke.

"I have to recount to you," he said, "a little history. I cannot tell you all the details, no. But I can give you the main outline. It concerns a young princeling who came to this country. He brought with him a famous jewel which he was to have reset for the lady he was going to marry, but unfortunately before that he made friends with a very pretty young lady. This pretty young lady did not care very much for the man, but she did care for his jewel–so much so that one day she disappeared with this historic possession which had belonged to his house for generations. So the poor young man, he is in a quandary, you see. Above all he cannot have a scandal. Impossible to go to the police. Therefore he comes to me, to Hercule Poirot. "Recover for me," he says, "my historic ruby." Eh bien, this young lady, she has a friend, and the friend, he has put through several very questionable transactions. He has been concerned with blackmail and he has been concerned with the sale of jewellery abroad. Always he has been very clever. He is suspected, yes, but nothing can be proved. It comes to my knowledge that this very clever gentleman, he is spending Christmas here in this house. It is important that the pretty young lady, once she has acquired the jewel, should disappear for a while from circulation, so that no pressure can be put upon her, no questions can be asked her. It is arranged, therefore, that she comes here to Kings Lacey, ostensibly as the sister of the clever gentleman–"

Sarah drew a sharp breath. "Oh, no. Oh, no, not here! Not with me here!"

"But so it is," said Poirot. "And by a little manipulation I, too, become a guest here for Christmas. This young lady, she is supposed to have just come out of hospital. She is much better when she arrives here. But then comes the news that I, too, arrive, a detective–a well-known detective. At once she has what you call the wind up. She hides the ruby in the first place she can think of, and then very quickly she has a relapse and takes to her bed again. She does not want that I should see her, for doubtless I have a photograph and I shall recognize her. It is very boring for her, yes, but she has to stay in her room and her brother, he brings her up the trays."

"And the ruby?" demanded Michael.

"I think," said Poirot, "that at the moment it is mentioned I arrive, the young lady was in the kitchen with the rest of you, all laughing and talking and stirring the Christmas puddings. The Christmas puddings are put into bowls and the young lady she hides the ruby, pressing it down into one of the pudding bowls. Not the one that we are going to have on Christmas Day. Oh no, that one she knows is in a special mould. She put it in the other one, the one that is destined to be eaten on New Year"s Day. Before then she will be ready to leave, and when she leaves no doubt that Christmas pudding will go with her. But see how fate takes a hand. On the very morning of Christmas Day there is an accident. The Christmas pudding in its fancy mould is dropped on the stone floor and the mould is shattered to pieces. So what can be done? The good Mrs Ross, she takes the other pudding and sends it in."

"Good lord," said Colin, "do you mean that on Christmas Day when Grandfather was eating his pudding that that was a real ruby he'd got in his mouth?"

"Precisely," said Poirot, "and you can imagine the emotions of Mr Desmond Lee-Wortley when he saw that. Eh bien, what happens next? The ruby is passed round. I examine it and I manage unobtrusively to slip it in my pocket. In a careless way as though I were not interested. But one person at least observes what I have done. When I lie in bed that person searches my room. He searches me. He does not find the ruby. Why?"

"Because," said Michael breathlessly, "you had given it to Bridget. That's what you mean. And so that's why–but I don't understand quite–I mean–Look here, what did happen?"

Poirot smiled at him.

"Come now into the library," he said, "and look out of the window and I will show you something that may explain the mystery."

He led the way and they followed him.

"Consider once again," said Poirot, "the scene of the crime."

He pointed out of the window. A simultaneous gasp broke from the lips of all of them. There was no body lying on the snow, no trace of the tragedy seemed to remain except a mass of scuffled snow.

"It wasn't all a dream, was it?" said Colin faintly. "I–has someone taken the body away?"

"Ah," said Poirot. "You see? The Mystery of the Disappearing Body." He nodded his head and his eyes twinkled gently.

"Good lord," cried Michael. "M. Poirot, you are–you haven't–oh, look here, he's been having us on all this time!"

Poirot twinkled more than ever.

"It is true, my children, I also have had my little joke. I knew about your little plot, you see, and so I arranged a counter-plot of my own. Ah, voilà Mademoiselle Bridget. None the worse, I hope, for your exposure in the snow? Never should I forgive myself if you attrapped une fluxion de poitrine."

Bridget had just come into the room. She was wearing a thick skirt and a woollen sweater. She was laughing.

"I sent a tisane to your room," said Poirot severely. "You have drunk it?"

"One sip was enough!" said Bridget. "I "m all right. Did I do it well, M. Poirot? Goodness, my arm hurts still after that tourniquet you made me put on it."

"You were splendid, my child," said Poirot. "Splendid. But see, all the others are still in the fog. Last night I went to

Mademoiselle Bridget. I told her that I knew about your little complot and I asked her if she would act a part for me. She did it very cleverly. She made the footprints with a pair of Mr Lee-Wortley"s shoes."

Sarah said in a harsh voice: "But what's the point of it all, M. Poirot? What's the point of sending Desmond off to fetch the police? They'll be very angry when they find out it's nothing but a hoax."

Poirot shook his head gently.

"But I do not think for one moment, Mademoiselle, that Mr Lee-Wortley went to fetch the police," he said. "Murder is a thing in which Mr Lee-Wortley does not want to be mixed up. He lost his nerve badly. All he could see was his chance to get the ruby. He snatched that, he pretended the telephone was out of order and he rushed off in a car on the pretence of fetching the police. I think myself it is the last you will see of him for some time. He has, I understand, his own ways of getting out of England. He has his own plane, has he not, Mademoiselle?"

Sarah nodded. "Yes," she said. "We were thinking of–" She stopped.

"He wanted you to elope with him that way, did he not? Eh bien, that is a very good way of smuggling a jewel out of the country. When you are eloping with a girl, and that fact is publicized, then you will not be suspected of also smuggling a historic jewel out of the country. Oh yes, that would have made a very good camouflage."

"I don't believe it," said Sarah. "I don't believe a word of it!"

"Then ask his sister," said Poirot, gently nodding his head over her shoulder. Sarah turned her head sharply.

A platinum blonde stood in the doorway. She wore a fur coat and was scowling. She was clearly in a furious temper.

"Sister my foot!" she said, with a short unpleasant laugh. "That swine's no brother of mine! So he's beaten it, has he, and left me to carry the can? The whole thing was his idea! He put me up to it! Said it was money for jam. They'd never prosecute because of the scandal. I could always threaten to say that Ali had given me his historic jewel. Des and I were to have shared the swag in Paris–and now the swine runs out on me! I'd like to murder him!" She switched abruptly. "The sooner I get out of here–Can someone telephone for a taxi?"

"A car is waiting at the front door to take you to the station, Mademoiselle," said Poirot.

"Think of everything, don"t you?"

"Most things," said Poirot complacently.

But Poirot was not to get off so easily. When he returned to the diningroom after assisting the spurious Miss Lee-Wortley into the waiting car, Colin was waiting for him. There was a frown on his boyish face.

"But look here, M. Poirot. What about the ruby? Do you mean to say you've let him get away with it?"

Poirot"s face fell. He twirled his moustaches. He seemed ill at ease. "I shall recover it yet," he said weakly. "There are other ways. I shall still–"

"Well, I do think!" said Michael. "To let that swine get away with the ruby!"

Bridget was sharper.

"He's having us on again," she cried. "You are, aren't you, M. Poirot?"

"Shall we do a final conjuring trick, Mademoiselle? Feel in my left-hand pocket."

Bridget thrust her hand in. She drew it out again with a scream of triumph and held aloft a large ruby blinking in crimson splendour.

"You comprehend," explained Poirot, "the one that was clasped in your hand was a paste replica. I brought it from London in case it was possible to make a substitute. You understand? We do not want the scandal. Monsieur Desmond will try and dispose of that ruby in Paris or in Belgium or wherever it is that he has his contacts, and then it will be discovered that the stone is not real! What could be more excellent? All finishes happily. The scandal is avoided, my princeling receives his ruby back again, he returns to his country and makes a sober and we hope a happy marriage. All ends well."

"Except for me," murmured Sarah under her breath. She spoke so low that no one heard her but Poirot. He shook his head gently.

"You are in error, Mademoiselle Sarah, in what you say there. You have gained experience. All experience is valuable. Ahead of you I prophesy there lies happiness."

"That's what you say," said Sarah.

"But look here, M. Poirot." Colin was frowning. "How did you know about the show we were going to put on for you?"

"It is my business to know things," said Hercule Poirot. He twirled his moustache.

"Yes, but I don"t see how you could have managed it. Did someone split–did someone come and tell you?"

"No, no, not that."

"Then how? Tell us how?"

They all chorused, "Yes, tell us how."

"But no," Poirot protested. "But no. If I tell you how I deduced that, you will think nothing of it. It is like the conjurer who shows how his tricks are done!"

"Tell us, M. Poirot! Go on. Tell us, tell us!"

"You really wish that I should solve for you this last mystery?"

"Yes, go on. Tell us."

"Ah, I do not think I can. You will be so disappointed."

"Now, come on, M. Poirot, tell us. How did you know?"

"Well, you see, I was sitting in the library by the window in a chair after tea the other day and I was reposing myself. I had been asleep and when I awoke you were discussing your plans just outside the window close to me, and the window was open at the top."

"Is that all?" cried Colin, disgusted. "How simple!"

"Is it not?" said Hercule Poirot, smiling. "You see? You are disappointed!"

"Oh well," said Michael, "at any rate we know everything now."

"Do we?" murmured Hercule Poirot to himself. "I do not. I, whose business it is to know things."

He walked out into the hall, shaking his head a little. For perhaps the twentieth time he drew from his pocket a rather dirty piece of paper.

"DON"T EAT NONE OF THE PLUM PUDDING. ONE AS WISHES YOU WELL.""

Hercule Poirot shook his head reflectively. He who could explain everything could not explain this! Humiliating. Who had written it? Why had it been written? Until he found that out he would never know a moment"s peace. Suddenly he came out of his reverie to be aware of a peculiar gasping noise. He looked sharply down. On the floor, busy with a dustpan and brush was a tow-headed creature in a flowered overall. She was staring at the paper in his hand with large round eyes.

"Oh sir," said this apparition. "Oh, sir. Please, sir."

"And who may you be, mon enfant?" inquired M. Poirot genially.

"Annie Bates, sir, please sir. I come here to help Mrs Ross. I didn't mean, sir, I didn't mean to–to do anything what I shouldn't do. I did mean it well, sir. For your good, I mean."

Enlightenment came to Poirot. He held out the dirty piece of paper.

"Did you write that, Annie?"

"I didn't mean any harm, sir. Really I didn't."

"Of course you didn't, Annie." He smiled at her. "But tell me about it. Why did you write this?"

"Well, it was them two, sir. Mr Lee-Wortley and his sister. Not that she was his sister, I'm sure. None of us thought so! And she wasn't ill a bit. We could all tell that. We thought– we all thought–something queer was going on. I'll tell you straight, sir. I was in her bathroom taking in the clean towels, and I listened at the door. He was in her room and they were talking together. I heard what they said plain as plain. "This detective," he was saying. "This fellow Poirot who's coming here. We've got to do something about it. We've got to get him out of the way as soon as possible." And then he says to her in a nasty, sinister sort of way, lowering his voice, "Where did you put it?" And she answered him, "In the pudding." Oh, sir, my heart gave such a leap I thought it would stop beating. I thought they meant to poison you in the Christmas pudding. I didn't know what to do! Mrs Ross, she wouldn't listen to the likes of me. Then the idea came to me as I'd write you a warning. And I did and I put it on your pillow where you'd find it when you went to bed." Annie paused breathlessly.

Poirot surveyed her gravely for some minutes.

"You see too many sensational films, I think, Annie," he said at last, "or perhaps it is the television that affects you? But the important thing is that you have the good heart and a certain amount of ingenuity. When I return to London I will send you a present."

"Oh thank you, sir. Thank you very much, sir."

"What would you like, Annie, as a present?"

"Anything I like, sir? Could I have anything I like?"

"Within reason," said Hercule Poirot prudently, "yes."

"Oh sir, could I have a vanity box? A real posh slap-up vanity box like the one Mr Lee-Wortley's sister, wot wasn't his sister, had?"

"Yes," said Poirot, "yes, I think that could be managed."

"It is interesting," he mused. "I was in a museum the other day observing some antiquities from Babylon or one of those places, thousands of years old–and among them were cosmetic boxes. The heart of woman does not change."

"Beg your pardon, sir?" said Annie.

"It is nothing," said Poirot. "I reflect. You shall have your vanity box, child."

"Oh thank you, sir. Oh thank you very much indeed, sir."

Annie departed ecstatically. Poirot looked after her, nodding his head in satisfaction.

"Ah," he said to himself. "And now–I go. There is nothing more to be done here."

A pair of arms slipped round his shoulders unexpectedly.

"If you will stand just under the mistletoe –" said Bridget.

VI

Hercule Poirot enjoyed it. He enjoyed it very much. He said to himself that he had had a very good Christmas.

Made in the USA
Middletown, DE
09 September 2024

60564095R00035